THE HAPPY RAG

D0352218

This paperback edition first published in 2001 by Andersen Press Ltd. All rights reserved.
The rights of Tony Ross to be identified as the author and illustrator of this work have been asserted by him
in accordance with the Copyright, Designs and Patents Act, 1988. Copyright ©1990 by Tony Ross.
First published in Great Britain in 1990 by Andersen Press Ltd., 20 Vauxhall Bridge Road, London SW1V 2SA.
Published in Australia by Random House Australia Pty., 20 Alfred Street, Milsons Point, Sydney, NSW 2061.
Colour separated in Switzerland by Photolitho AG, Zurich.Printed and bound in Italy by Grafiche AZ, Verona.

10 9 8 7 6 5 4 3 2

British Library Cataloguing in Publication Data available.

ISBN 1 84270 053 7

This book has been printed on acid-free paper

THE HAPPY RAG

This paperback edition first published in 2001 by Andersen Press Ltd. All rights reserved.
The rights of Tony Ross to be identified as the author and illustrator of this work have been asserted by him
in accordance with the Copyright, Designs and Patents Act, 1988. Copyright ©1990 by Tony Ross.
First published in Great Britain in 1990 by Andersen Press Ltd., 20 Vauxhall Bridge Road, London SW1V 2SA.
Published in Australia by Random House Australia Pty., 20 Alfred Street, Milsons Point, Sydney, NSW 2061.
Colour separated in Switzerland by Photolitho AG, Zurich.Printed and bound in Italy by Grafiche AZ, Verona.

10 9 8 7 6 5 4 3 2

British Library Cataloguing in Publication Data available.

ISBN 1 84270 053 7

This book has been printed on acid-free paper

THE HAPPY RAG

Tony Ross

Andersen Press • London

Lucy was afraid of nearly everything.

Spiders in the bath ...

... dark shadows and things on T.V.

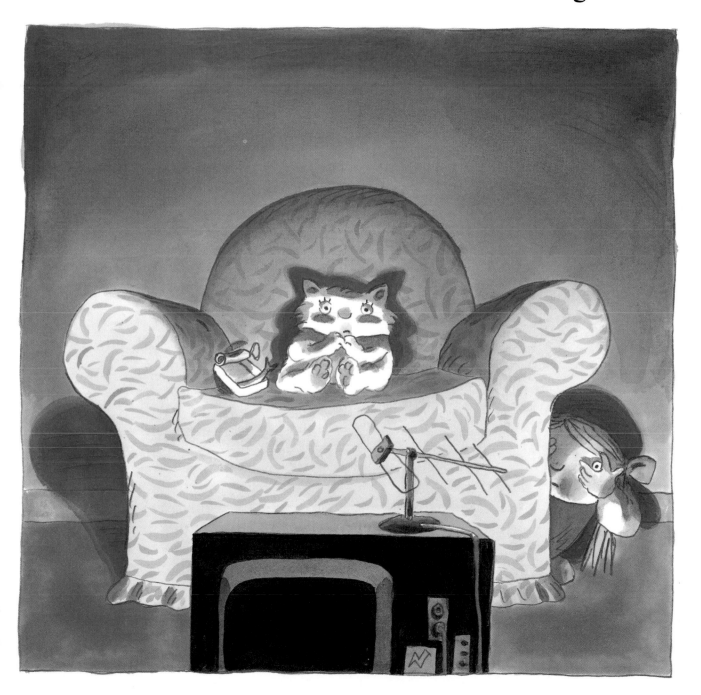

... that she just had to watch.

Then one day, Lucy found a happy rag,

and then she felt safe.

Her happy rag looked after her all the time,

even when she was asleep.

Once, Dad took her rag away

and threw it in the dustbin. ("Dirty old thing," he said.)

But Lucy took it back again.

"It's the big growly bear who looks after me," she said.

Once, Mum tried to take her rag away.

"It's ready for the wash!" she said.

"No!" said Lucy.

"It's the big growly bear who looks after me."

So Lucy took her big growly bear to the park

where nobody would put him into the washing machine.

Suddenly, around a corner, she heard a dreadful noise.

"Yeeeeeeeeerr!" it went. "Woooooooooo!" went Lucy.

"It must be something dreadful,"

"Grrrrrrrr! Grrrrrrrr!"

cried Lucy. "Woooooooooohh! HELP!"

went her big growly bear.

And the bear chased away a magician

from the claws of a big growly bear.

on a wonderful flying carpet.

And the magic carpet saved him

cried Gregory. "Yeeeeeeeerr!HELP!

... on my magic carpet."

"It must be something terrible,"

I'd better be off ...

Suddenly, around a corner, he heard a terrible noise.

"Woooooooooohh!" it went. "Yeeeeeeeeerr!" went Gregory.

When the dragon was dead

Gregory went for a walk in the park.

"It's not a gooey old blanket. It's a suit of armour,"

said Gregory, waving his sword at a dragon.

"Don't you think you are a bit old for a gooey old blanket?

Only babies have those," said Uncle Sid.

"It's not a dirty old thing!" said Gregory. "It's a pirate ship."

And he sailed south to the Spanish Main.

"You shouldn't put that dirty old thing in your mouth.

It's bad for you and your nose may fall off," said Grandpa.

And he zoomed out to play in the stars.

"It isn't a yucky old rag," said Gregory, "It's a spaceship."

It makes you look silly," said awful Aunt Maggie.

"You shouldn't go out with that yucky old rag!

Although Gregory wasn't afraid of the dark,

he was even less afraid of it when he had his happy rag.

He called it his happy rag.

Gregory had a rag that made him feel happy.

Andersen Press • London

Tony Ross

THE HAPPY RAG